MARGRET & H.A. REY'S

Curious George

and the Sleepover

Written by Monica Perez

Illustrated in the style of H. A. Rey by Anna Grossnickle Hines

Houghton Mifflin Harcourt

Boston   New York

For Julian Perez-Reyzin, my latest love. —M.P.

For Linnea and Arden Mae. —A.H.

www.hmhco.com

The text type was set in Garamond.

ISBN 978-0-544-76346-3

Manufactured in China
SCP 10 9 8 7 6 5 4 3 2 1
4500615007

George is a good little monkey and always very curious.

George's curiosity helped him make friends everywhere.
Tallulah and Jarrod were his good friends from down the
street. They lived with their dad and Gramma Willa.

On weekends they
liked to spend time
together. Gramma Willa
took them swimming,
to the zoo, or to the park.

One day, Jarrod had some news. "My dad is leaving this weekend for a work trip. Gramma is planning a special fun night on Saturday! We get to watch a movie, eat popcorn with real butter, and go to bed half an hour late."

Tallulah added, "Gramma says you can spend the night with us, and in the morning we can make waffles!"

A sleepover sounded wonderful to George. The man with the yellow hat agreed to the plan. Hooray!

It was only Wednesday, so George had plenty of time to prepare for his first sleepover. He was curious about his new sleeping bag, so he tried it out.

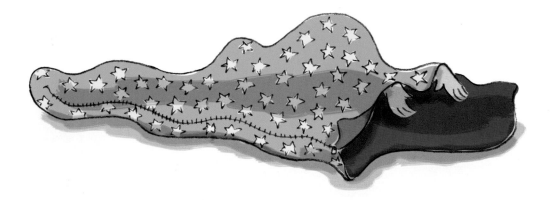

On Thursday he borrowed the man's backpack. He would need his toothbrush, his pajamas, his alarm clock with the bird that chirped on top, a flashlight . . . and snacks!

On Friday, George had to pack more snacks because he had eaten all the bananas in the bag.

Then he packed two suitcases full of toys. His friend suggested that George might want to travel with less . . . so George settled on taking his favorite toy, Lola.

On Saturday, George was still excited, but a funny feeling had begun to settle in the pit of his stomach . . . It started out small, as if maybe George had eaten too many cookies. But as the day wore on, the feeling began to grow.

"Are you excited, George?" the man asked.
Perhaps George was a little excited. He was a little nervous, too!

The doorbell rang. Tallulah and Jarrod burst through the door, chattering away about their plans for the evening. They had made George a red sash with blue letters that said "Guest of Honor"!

For a moment, George forgot about being worried.
He proudly wore the sash down the street and into his
friends' house. Even when it came time for George to say
goodbye to the man with the yellow hat, George didn't
remember he had been nervous, because he was helping
Tallulah set up a tent in the living room.

George and his friends
had a busy evening.
They watched a movie
and ate popcorn.

They had a pillow fight.

When it was time for
bed, they brushed their
teeth, changed into
PJs, and climbed into
the tent. Tallulah and
Jarrod fell right
to sleep.

But George didn't. The floor was a little hard.
He missed his bed at home. He stared at the shadows
on the ceiling of the tent. Was that a bear?

George's stomach did a little flip. He peeked out the tent flap and saw that it was only the coat rack casting shadows on the tent. He settled back onto his pillow. But then he heard a soft scratching sound.

He jumped out of the tent with Lola safely in hand. He looked out the window and saw the branches of an apple tree scratching the side of the house. How silly of him to worry!

George had an idea. He would make himself some warm milk.
That always helped him sleep at home.

George poured himself a mug of milk. Oops. He would have
to clean that spill up later. He wasn't quite sure how to go
about warming up the milk. He knew not to touch the stove.

At home, his friend always heated the milk for him. So George just arranged some cookies on a plate. Yum—they would go nicely with the milk.

But holding on to a full mug and the cookies was hard work. He spilled more milk onto the floor.

George put down the cookies and went looking for a mop.
There it was. Oh, no! He accidentally swiped the mop across
the table. Cookies went flying!

George wished he were at home with the man there to help. He didn't want to wake up his friends. If he got a sponge from the sink maybe he could clean up the spill. But as he hurried across the kitchen, he slipped on the wet floor.

Poor George. Now he was homesick *and* wet. He started to sniffle.

The light in the kitchen went on. Gramma Willa scooped George and Lola up. She gave them a hug and dried them off. Then Gramma called the man with the yellow hat so George could hear his voice.

Tallulah and Jarrod woke up too and helped cheer George up.

"I was nervous about spending a night away from home at my first sleepover too," Tallulah confessed.

"Not me," Jarrod said proudly.

"That's because you haven't gone to one yet," Tallulah said.

"Have too. This one!" insisted Jarrod. Tallulah and George just smiled.

George felt better. He snuggled down into the sleeping bag that Gramma spread on the living room couch. The kids pulled their sleeping bags out of the tent and spread them on the floor near George. Gramma left a small light on over the desk. They all fell right to sleep.

And in the morning, George helped make
banana and chocolate chip waffles for breakfast.

When the man came to pick George up, he heard all about how fun the sleepover had been. George and the man thanked their friends and waved goodbye.

"So, George. Do you think you'll be ready for another sleepover sometime?" the man asked.

George was already packing for it!